BEAST HUNT

Jillian Powell

Illustrated by David Lupton

Ginn

"A farm?" Tod looked horrified.

"A farm holiday," said Mum. "It will be lovely and peaceful. Just what we need."

"Will there be baby lambs?" asked Amy.

Tod rolled his eyes. His little sister Amy was mad about fluffy animals.

"Lots of lambs," said Mum, "and chickens too. Just think – fresh eggs for breakfast!"

Great, thought Tod. He was spending his holidays on a smelly old farm. His mate Leigh was flying off to Spain. Leigh was staying at a hotel that had a pool with a water chute, while Tod was going to be knee-deep in cowpats.

In fact, there were no cows. But that was as good as it got. It was raining when they arrived.

"Welcome to Sunnybrook Farm!" Mrs Langley showed them in.

Rainybrook Farm more like, thought Tod.

Tod looked round. Did the sun ever shine here?

The big old farmhouse was in the middle of nowhere.

There were no other houses, just trees and fields with sheep in them. The farmyard was full of sticky mud. Tod had ruined his new trainers just getting out of the car.

"Can we go see the lambs?" asked Amy.

"Tomorrow," said Mum. "There's plenty of time. We've got two whole weeks, remember?"

Tod's heart sank. Two weeks on a smelly old farm. Thank goodness he'd brought his computer games.

The next day, the sun was shining. Tod had breakfast with Mum, Amy and Mrs Langley's fat ginger cat and two dogs. The dogs stared at him as he ate. They looked as if they might jump up and grab his bacon.

After breakfast, Mrs Langley took Mum and Amy to see the chickens. Pass, thought Tod. Leigh was probably checking out the beach in Spain right now. Tod went outside to play with his football. On the way to the field, he passed the lambing shed. The door was open, and there was a strong, sweet smell of hay.

Tod heard two voices.

"I hear there was another killing last night," one said.

"Yes, over at Ley's Farm," the other said. "It's all over the newspapers."

"Don says they're calling in the Marines," the first voice said. "A crack team of commandos."

Tod stood frozen to the spot. A killer on the loose! This holiday just got a whole lot better.

Tod heard footsteps behind him. It was the newspaper boy.

"Hello, mate. Are you staying here? D'you want to take this in?" He handed Tod a newspaper.

Mrs Langley was still out with Mum and Amy. Tod went indoors and unfolded the paper. He wanted to find out about the killer.

Tod read the article.

A mystery beast that was killing sheep in the area had struck again. A hundred sheep and lambs had been killed in eight months. The farmer at Ley's Farm had found a dead lamb in the fields, with its bones licked clean.

No one knew what the beast was. Some local people thought it was a wild dog.

The newspaper offered a £5000 reward for anyone who could help catch the beast.

That night, Tod found it hard to sleep. He lay awake, thinking about the beast. It was past midnight when he heard men talking outside his window.

Tod slipped out of bed and peeped through the window. Mr Langley was out in the farmyard with a group of other farmers. They were carrying torches and shotguns.

"We'll work in pairs," said Mr Langley. "We don't know how big this thing is, or how dangerous. And remember, it can run fast. Don said it outran his Land Rover easily the other night."

The men headed out into the fields, talking quietly together. Tod climbed back into bed. He couldn't help wishing he was out there with them.

4

The next morning, Tod was the first down to breakfast. Mr and Mrs Langley were talking in the kitchen.

"Right under our noses," Mr Langley was saying. "I don't understand it. We kept watch all night, and it still took a lamb from right under our noses."

They heard Tod coming down, and quickly stopped talking.

"Good morning, young man," said Mrs Langley, brightly. "Are you ready for a full English breakfast?"

"Please," Tod nodded.

"What are you up to today?" she asked, bustling about with jugs of milk and juice.

"I thought I might go into the village," said Tod. "I need a new battery for my computer game."

"Oh yes. Well, that's an easy walk, straight along the lane. No need to go into the woods. You might get lost!" said Mrs Langley, smiling.

You might get eaten, more like, thought Tod. He could tell Mrs Langley didn't want to talk about the beast. It probably wasn't much good for farm holidays, having a killer beast on the loose.

Tod wanted to see if he could find out any more about the beast hunt while he was in the village.

The Post Office had a sign in the window.

"I've seen it, you know," a girl's voice said behind him. Tod turned round.

Help us catch the BEAST!
Check your outbuildings every day.
Ring this number, if you see the BEAST.
Tel: 543678

A teenage girl was standing there eating an ice cream.

"I was out riding," she told Tod. "I saw this thing running along the hedgerow, like it was hunting something. The barley was really high, but I could see this great big, thick neck. It looked massive. Bigger than a dog. Wish I'd had my camera," she added. "Might have got five grand!"

"What do you think it is?" Tod asked the girl.

She shrugged. "Ask Beevis. He's the man," she said. "You get these in there, by the way," she said, nodding at her ice cream.

Pass, thought Tod. He was still really full after his breakfast. Besides, he had more important things than ice cream on his mind.

5

"What do you want to do today?" Mum asked Tod the next day. "Amy wants to go to the doll museum in the village."

"I'll just hang around here," said Tod. He kept thinking about the newspaper reward. If he could just get a shot of the beast with his camera …

"Okay," said Mum, "but don't wander further than the woods, and don't get under Mr Langley's feet."

Tod set off towards the woods. Sheep were grazing in the fields. Birds were singing. It was hardly the place to find a killer, thought Tod. Then he spotted something. There was a tuft of black fur on the wire fence. Tod pulled it off and examined it.

Suddenly, he heard a noise behind him. Leaves rustled and twigs crackled underfoot. Tod held his breath.

"What've you got there?" a gruff voice asked.

Tod turned to see a man watching him. "I … I wondered if it was the beast's." stammered Tod.

"Of course it's the beast's," said the man.

"Are you one of the Marines?" asked Tod.

"Load of nonsense, commandos and Marines," the man told him. "You need someone who knows the country to catch this thing. There isn't a man alive who knows these woods better than me. Name's Beevis, by the way."

"What do you think this thing is then?" asked Tod.

"Come with me," said Beevis. Tod watched Beevis walk off into one of the fields, unsure if he should follow him. Then again, there was a killer somewhere out there, and Beevis seemed like the man to find it. Tod ran to catch Beevis up.

"A lamb was killed in this field last night," Beevis told Tod. "Now, when a dog gets into a field, the sheep panic and bunch up. If this thing were a wild dog, you'd see the marks in the mud. But, look. Nothing worried these sheep last night."

"But, but a lamb was killed!" said Tod.

Beevis nodded.

"Then what … ?"

"Have you ever been tracking?" asked Beevis.

Tod shook his head.

"Let's see if we can find you your first track, then," said Beevis.

It seemed as if they had been creeping around in the fields for hours. Tod was getting bored and hungry when Beevis suddenly stopped.

"Look!"

There were tracks in the mud.

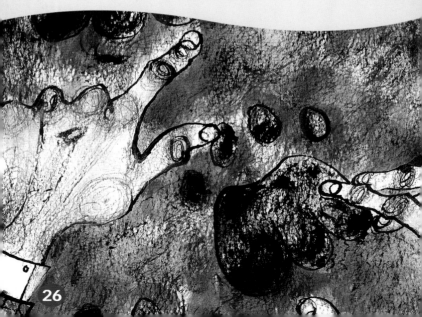

"Mud or wet sand," Beevis told Tod. "That's the best place to find tracks like these."

"What are they?" asked Tod. He crouched down beside Beevis.

"See that – the way it's split in two?" asked Beevis. "That's not a wild dog's print."

"It's big!" said Tod.

"What else can you see?"

Tod got closer.

"Claws?"

"That's it. Now, some people might think it's a dog, because a cat walks with its claws in, like this," Beevis curled the fingers of his hand. "The only big cat that doesn't pull its claws in is the cheetah, and it's not one of those – unless someone has painted it black!" said Beevis.

"But, if you look closely, these claws are sharp, not blunt like a dog's. It looks like a cat gripping onto wet mud."

Tod put out his hand to touch the print.

"Don't do that!" Beevis stopped him.

"We need to make a cast before the rain washes it away."

Beevis opened his bag and took out some cardboard, a bag of plaster, and a bottle of water.

"We need to make a frame first," he told Tod. "Put this cardboard round the track, see?"

Tod pushed the strips of cardboard into the mud, being careful not to get too close to the print.

Beevis was mixing together the plaster and water.

"Now we pour this in, and wait for it to set hard," he told Tod. "Then we'll have our cast. It should give us a few more clues about what this beast really is."

Tod couldn't wait to see the cast. The next day, he asked his mum if he could go for a walk again, and set off for Beevis' place. Beevis lived on the edge of the woods. It was more like a hut than a house. Tod found him indoors. A huge black dog was asleep at his feet.

"He's miserable," said Beevis, nodding at the dog. "He can't go out, you see."

"Surely the beast wouldn't … "

"Not the beast," said Beevis. "The Marines or the farmers. There are some daft rumours, you see. Some of the locals are saying the beast is a poacher's dog that's being trained to kill."

"Are you a poacher?" asked Tod.

Beevis didn't answer him.

"I told you, it's not a dog," he snapped. "Dogs attack sheep from behind. They grab the legs and pull the sheep down. This thing attacks at the neck. Then it licks the bones clean."

Tod could see the cast of the paw print on a table. There were three others like it. There were also several glass jars containing black fur.

"I sent that off to a lab," Beevis told Tod. "It's cat's fur all right. But this is no ordinary moggie."

Beevis showed Tod a map on the wall. It had red dots showing where the beast had been seen.

"This thing can run," Beevis told Tod. "It's been seen in two places, twenty miles apart, in the same day."

"Wow!" said Tod.

"There's something else." Beevis said. "Something I want you to hear. But not in here, or we'll upset Fangs," he nodded at the sleeping dog.

Tod followed Beevis outside. Beevis had a tape recorder. He turned it on, and it played a sound that turned Tod's blood to ice.

"That's what our beast sounds like. It's a real jungle scream, isn't it?" Beevis said. "Others have heard it, mostly at night. They say animals go mad when they hear it. Horses bolt. Dogs break loose from their leads … "

"It sounded like it was really close," said Tod.

"My plan is to get the beast a lot closer. Close enough to trap," Beevis told Tod. "First we need to dig a pit and rig up a trap," he explained. "Then I'll play the tape.

The beast will hear it and come to investigate. Cats are territorial, you see. If it thinks it's got a rival, it will come to see it off. Then, hey presto, we've bagged it!"

"Excellent!" Tod punched the air. "When do we do it?"

"We?" Beevis shook his head. "No way, Tod. It's too dangerous. You can help with the pit if you like. But I'll be playing the tape alone, tomorrow night."

"That's not fair!" Tod kicked the ground.

"Here, take a spade. You can help me set the trap – and then if we get the reward, I'll share it with you." Beevis promised.

Tod followed Beevis out into the woods. It was hard work digging the pit. When it was big enough, Beevis laid a huge net over the hole. Then he told Tod to cover it with leaves and branches.

"Now, you go back to your mum and sister," Beevis told Tod. "You can come back in the morning. I'm going to take Fangs over to the next valley for a walk. The poor thing is miserable, stuck indoors."

9

The door to the hut was open and Tod crept inside. The tape recorder was on the table. Tod put it in his bag with his camera. Mum would probably kill him. Beevis too. Tod knew that what he was doing was wrong, but if he could just get a shot with his camera … something to show Leigh. Otherwise no one would ever believe him. Beevis had got him hooked on this beast hunt. It wasn't fair to shut him out now.

Tod went deep into the woods. For his hideout, Tod scrambled up into the branches of a big old tree and settled down. Then he took out the tape recorder, and pressed 'Play'.

The blood-curdling scream rang out into the woods. Rooks scattered overhead like gunshot. Then it was silent.

Tod waited a while, but nothing happened, so he rewound the tape and played it again.

A scream rang out. But this time it wasn't the tape. The beast was nearby! Tod sat tight in the tree, his heart racing. What if this thing could climb trees? He was beginning to think he should have gone home after all.

Just then, Tod heard something moving below. He looked down and saw a huge black cat moving in the bushes. Its neck was massive. Its long tail lashed the trees. Tod was terrified. He almost cried out, but then he remembered why he was there. He had to get a picture to show Leigh.

Tod's hands were shaking as he took out his camera.

The flash lit up the woods, and the beast looked up at Tod. It snarled, showing sharp white teeth. Tod's heart was thumping. The beast crouched down on its back legs, and stared up at Tod. It looked exactly like a cat getting ready to jump, only much bigger, and much more terrifying.

Tod froze – there was nothing he could do. He couldn't climb down the tree with the beast prowling around, but if he stayed in the tree the beast would surely climb up and get him. The beast moved further back on its haunches, preparing to jump. Tod watched in terror, as it started to spring up … then, suddenly, it vanished! It was almost as if the ground had swallowed it up.

"I don't understand it," Beevis said to Tod the next morning.

"It must have been pure luck. That it fell into the trap like that, and in daylight too."

Tod knew it wasn't luck, but he tried not to let it show. "We set a good trap," Tod said proudly. "And we make a good picture too!"

They were admiring the photo on the front page of the newspaper. It showed Tod and Beevis standing alongside an animal cage, with the beast snarling inside.

"They think it's an unknown species, you know," Beevis told Tod.

"A wild cat, crossed with something that escaped from a zoo," said Beevis.

"They should name it after us," Tod grinned. "A Beetod, or a Todvis, or something!"

"You'd better take this newspaper home with you," Beevis said. "Or your friends are never going to believe you!"

"Right," said Tod. One thing was certain. He just couldn't wait to show Leigh his holiday snaps.